FATAL ATTRACTION

Written By

Arlin Couch

Table of Contents

Flashback of Monday, October 11th, 2021

Monday, October 11th, 2021, at approximately 6:37 a.m., Michael Michaelson had just walked into the College Of Southern Nevada library located in Henderson, Nevada, earlier than usual when he noticed Mrs. Niko's feet and ankles sticking out from behind a bookshelf. He immediately ran down the aisle hastily, hoping he wasn't about to run up on his favorite librarian harmed in any manner.

Michael reached the aisle Mrs. Niko was in and found her fine and dandy, just searching for something in the floor. "Thank God," he said to himself as he was trying to catch his breath from the start of a panic attack that was about to come on.

"Are you okay, Michael?" Mrs. Niko asked as she turned and saw him ghost faced and in a clammy manner.

"Yes," he said loudly with joy. "I came in and only saw your feet sticking out behind the bookshelf and I thought for sure I was going to walk upon a different scene."

Mrs. Niko stood up from the floor, body slightly shaking all over, clammy, and sweaty, took her left hand and gently stroked Michael's soft, pale cheeks and said, "Thank you, Michael, for actually caring enough to actually come and check on me, I am fine though, but were you needing something?" Mrs. Niko asked, kind of nervously.

"I'm kind of busy at the moment getting caught up on a couple of things before school starts." Michael said, "No, I was just returning my book."

"Why so early?" Mrs. Niko thought to herself as Michael started walking toward the slot in the desk in front of her office where you return your books. Mrs. Niko heard a noise coming from her office, so did Michael, "Did you hear that, Mrs. Niko?"

"Yes, that's just the air kicking on, just lay that book over here on the table, and I'll put that up for you, it will be easier for me to just put it back on the shelf since I'm already over here." Mrs. Niko slightly giggled after explaining.

Michael said, "Okay, sounds good," as he lay the book down on the old wobbly Cherry wood library table. Michael then walked off and left the library, kind of confused, but didn't say anything else. As soon as she heard the exit door shut, Mrs. Niko ran down the aisle towards the door and locked the deadbolt.

As soon as she locked the deadbolt she then began to dart towards her office. She unlocked and opened her office door, and there it was, the reasoning behind all of the nervousness, all of the anxiousness that she had been exerting all morning, "We have to go, we have to get out of here now! Drop everything, forget whatever you're doing" she said with a stern tone. But this isn't where the story starts.

Thursday, October 7th, 2021

Everyone in school knew Cooper Clarke, the blonde-wavy-haired, blue-eyed 20-year-old basketball Phenom in his sophomore year, the straight-A student, probably the most respected student to ever grace the campus of Southern Nevada Community College, and theirs very few people who wouldn't have agreed.

Everyone knew him as the kindhearted, give-you-the-shirt off of his back, unworldly athletic, the type of guy that a girl wants her parents to meet, a student who lived in the library. But what they didn't know about Cooper was that today, Thursday, October 7th, 2021, he would initiate a flirtatious conversation with the most beautiful blonde-headed college librarian, Mrs. Brandi Niko, that he would soon regret. Cooper was always a very friendly student. He didn't discriminate against race, gender, physical or mental disabilities was friends with everyone. When he wasn't on the basketball court dazzling the team fans with his impressive skills, he was either in class or in the library studying and doing homework, and that's how this whole situation got started.

Thursday, October 7th, 2021, it was a cool, beautiful fall day outside, but Cooper would rather admire it from a half-open window in the library beside where he always sat to study. Books weren't the only thing Cooper liked to look at and read in the library though, nor his favorite.

Mrs. Brandi Niko, the 42-year-old blonde-headed Wheel Herd librarian, was the most beautiful woman Cooper had ever laid eyes on. She would always be working on something in the library, whether it was putting returned books back on the shelf, checking books out for students, or simply just being there for a helping hand for any student in need. She always wore a tight, just above-the-knee, blue Levi or either black, tan, or smoke-gray skirt every day of the week. We most certainly can't forget that the skirt was always unmatched with a different colored button-up collared shirt, even though the colors of the shirt and skirt were unmatched, the colors always made each other pop out. She always had one or two of the top buttons unbuttoned just to show a little cleavage as well. The school faculty never complained about the cleavage Mrs. Niko never minded showing, maybe because their students, especially the males, spent a whole lot of time in there studying instead of just roaming campus doing nothing.

One student who admired her a tremendous amount more than others was none other than Cooper Clarke, who would spend every minute he could in that library ever since the first time he entered in during the first week of school back in August. The only difference about today than any other, was that Cooper had decided to try and flirt with Mrs. Niko a little bit just to see what her reaction would be at first.

Mrs. Niko was making a lap around the library, dusting the shelves, placing returned books back in their spaces, checking on all the students to make sure they didn't need any help, and so-on.

Mrs. Niko approached Cooper, this interaction would be a little different to the others. She made her way over beside Cooper's desk with her book cart and put a book on the shelf within arm's reach of Cooper. He heard the book rattle against the wooden shelf and turned around, "How are you doing this morning, Mrs. Niko?" he said with confidence and a smile that couldn't be hidden.

Mrs. Niko replied back, "I'm doing great Cooper! How are you doing today? I see you're working on something for history, maybe?"

Cooper explained, "Yes, I'm actually working on a report over World War I and about how I think it affected what the world is like today." She said, "Oh, that's interesting."

"Here's my chance to attempt to flirt with her and see if she takes the bait," Cooper thought to himself. "Yes, it is pretty interesting, but I doubt it's anywhere near as interesting as you are, Mrs. Niko." Cooper said discreetly to Mrs. Niko, kind of nervous of what her response would be.

Mrs. Niko giggled and said, "I don't know about that now, I live a pretty boring life."

"There's nothing boring about you, Mrs. Niko, I find an adventure in your beauty every time I look at you." Cooper said as he smiled and gave a wink with his left eye.

Mrs. Niko, trying to hold back a smile as the blood rushes to her face, turning it fire extinguisher red, just grinned and whispered, "Thanks, you don't know how much I appreciate a compliment, it's been awhile since I've had one from my husband."

"Well, I'll shut up after this remark," Cooper said quietly to Mrs. Niko, "But if I was your husband, you'd never need to want a compliment, but I had better get back to my work, you have a great rest of your day Mrs. Niko."

Mrs. Niko bit her bottom lip a tad with a twinkle in her eye and said, "You too, Cooper." Mrs. Niko walked off from where Cooper was sitting, pushing her cart still with a few more books to put back on the shelves, stopping and chatting with students along the way, of course, none of the chats comparing to the one she had just had with Cooper Clarke moments before.

As she stopped at the last bookshelf before her desk to put the last remaining returned book on it, she turned and gives one more look and smiled towards Cooper. He was actually putting all of his things back into his backpack, so he missed the last interaction. Cooper got all of his things into his bag, threw it over his left shoulder, and walked out of the library.

Friday, October 8th, 2021

Friday, October 8th, 2021, Mrs. Niko was sitting in the library behind her desk, checking books in, enjoying a slow Friday morning before the weekend. All of the students were being so nice and telling her she had a different glow about her today. She would smile and tell them she was just happy it was Friday, knowing that wasn't the real reason. She was really wishing it was Monday so Cooper Clarke would be back in the library studying.

As she sat at her desk, she couldn't help but to keep smiling as she kept reminiscing about her interaction with Cooper yesterday afternoon. Of course, she was thinking some sexual thoughts, especially when she was reminded that her husband hadn't touched her in bed in the past 6 months. She would think about if her and Cooper would be able to contain a dirty little secret like that if they were to pursue what they both knew each other were thinking, and if they did pursue and got caught, what would happen? But at the same time, she kept trying to shake the thoughts out of her head because of the fact that she knew what would happen, and it would not be good.

It was now 3:00 p.m., and Mrs. Niko's day was coming to a close in 15 minutes as she was roaming around the library with her cart, putting all of the returned books up, straightening all of the out-of-place books up on the shelves, and dusting her shelves, tables, and chairs getting them clean before the weekend. She finally grabs her purse, lunch bag, and new curriculum she has to look over to head home for the weekend.

So, Brandi Niko finally pulls into her driveway, turns the car off, sighs a deep breath, and just sits there silently, of course, with Cooper Clarke on her mind. It's now around 3:35 p.m., and Mr. Niko doesn't get home from work until about 6 o clock in the evening, so Brandi has close to 2 and a half hours of alone time.

As she sits in her vehicle still, yet she decides to scroll through her Facebook page to see what all her newsfeed has to offer. "Wow…" she said aloud to herself as she sees a post from her old college friend about how she's now single.

Now, thinking to herself, "How sometimes I wish I had the freedom of a single woman." She just sighs and scrolls on down the page, coming down to the "Friends you may know" section of Facebook. She decides to stop and see if she notices anybody. First-person, Jimmy Hart, "Name sounds familiar, but I don't know," she says to herself. She scrolls her screen over again swiftly with her right thumb. Anderson Newell,

"Hey, that's a student I had last year. Pretty cool."

"I would've never thought of seeing him on friends you may know." She scrolls through a few more recommendations, not knowing them at all unless she did and forgot. Then it came, the scroll that would make her jaw drop, Cooper Clarke! She looked around out of her car windows again to make sure her husband hadn't decided to surprisingly make it home early nope. Not even a jogger was passing by at the time. She was in the clear.

So she immediately clicked on his profile, she started looking at his information, same small town that she lived in, born December 6th, 2000, in her mind that was a date she kind of wanted to remember so she could be sure and tell him, he loves sports, reading, and hiking just like she does, and to her surprise, single. "Oh my God," she said aloud to herself, "I shouldn't be looking on his page, he's one of my students!" She clicked off of his page and began scrolling again through the wild world of Facebook, "Happy Birthday!" she wrote on Michelle, her old college roommate's page.

Back to scrolling, "hmm, Dave bought a new truck," she thought to herself as she scrolled past her husband's co-workers post, but still yet, she was still had Cooper on her mind. She couldn't bear it another second, she just had to check his page out.

So she began scrolling back up until she saw the "Friends You May Know" section again, scrolls over 5 or 6 times, and it was like the sunshine when his name showed up on the screen. Brandi clicked on his name, made it to the profile, and straight to the photo albums.

"I know I shouldn't be doing this, but he's of age, and I can't contain myself any longer," she said to herself as she clicked on the most recent Cooper Clarke photo album. She scrolls through the pictures, a few of him on the basketball court, a few of him and friends hanging out, and then all of a sudden, one of him with no shirt on with arms propped up on the door facing.

"Oh my God," she said to herself as she was admiring his ripped muscles and tan body. She just can't quit staring at the picture as takes her left hand down toward her female area to start rubbing herself through her panties under her skirt.

"Ah," she moans quietly in her car alone with her eyes closed. She hears a car from the distance and opens her eyes, pulls her hand back from between her thighs, clicks off of her students' page, grabs her bags and curriculum to run in the house.

She looks at the time on her phone: "4:10 p.m.," almost 2 hours still before Dean, Mr. Niko is supposed to be home. So, she decides to get back on Facebook and find Cooper once more. So she does, the only difference this time is she is in the bathroom alone where nobody can see her. She goes back to the same picture she was on and takes her hand right back to rubbing her vagina, only this time, the panties weren't in her way. As she's caressing herself, she can't hold her eyes open any longer because of how hot and bothered she is, she still has her phone in her hand, but by this time, she's about to get off and she's about to come right off the toilet seat.

This whole time she has been on Cooper's Facebook page, she finally gets composure of herself, calms down, lays her phone face down on the sink, washes her hands, then picks her phone back up and looks down at it to see a Facebook message from the one she was just fantasizing about Cooper Clarke. While she was doing the deed, her uncontrollable hand has sent a jumbled mess of a message to him, and he has replied!

"Oh my God," she said as she covers her mouth with her hand. "What have I done?" She paced back and forth in her bathroom, freaking out, wandering if she should open it and reply or just delete it and act like nothing happened. Of course, she can't take the suspense no longer, she decides to open the message.

Her message, "jeferutfwiw," made her feel like a lunatic, but his message, "Well, hello to you as well, good looking! Lol," with a winking emoji.

She gave a slight smile and messaged back, saying, "Oh no, I'm so sorry, that was an accident, I have no clue what that message is supposed to be!" She sat biting her nails, waiting on the read receipt to pop up, by this time, it's now 4:30 p.m., so she still has an hour and a half before her husband is supposed to get home from work. "Ding," her phone goes off, and it's Cooper.

"But you must have been on my page for you to be able to message me, lol, and now you have me intrigued," he sends jokingly.

Of course, though, Brandi smiles at the thought of him flirting, "Well, what if I was?" she sends back. Considering how he has spoken with her in the library, I think she knows where this is going to go.

"Messenger: Cooper Clarke" pops up across her phone screen and she can barely contain the excitement to open it.

"Well, were you pleasuring yourself to my profile? Ha-ha, just kidding," the message says.

Mrs. Niko sends back, "Let's be adults here, that's exactly what I was doing, and you're not 'Just kidding,' are you?" A surge of adrenaline ran through her whole body as she hit send, she even started sweating, pacing back and forth, still yet in the bathroom.

"Ding," phone goes off, "Messenger: Cooper Clarke," "No, not at all am I kidding." She is so relieved to know this.

She looks down at her phone, 4:50 p.m., she still has a little bit of time before her husband is home. So she decides to go for broke, she strips all of her clothes off, including the panties and bra, she stands in her doorway mirror, snaps a picture, and sends it straight on to Cooper. Again, she's biting her nails as she sees that he read it, and now she's awaiting a response.

"Ding," her phone goes off, and it's Cooper, "This is what I'm doing to that picture as we speak," another message from him comes through, it's a video.

Brandi opens the video, and it's Cooper masturbating. Brandi starts losing her breath and fantasizing as she's rubbing herself, she sets her camera up against the door in the floor presses record. She sits in the floor of the bathroom in front of her camera and records herself masturbating until she gets off. She finishes and then hits send to Cooper.

Cooper messages back, "This is the greatest video I've ever received. I'll keep it forever to use," with a wink face emoji at the end. Mrs.

Niko responds back, "No, you cannot keep that, you have to delete it. I could lose everything. Here, I'll delete yours as well."

She shows Cooper proof that his video is deleted, Cooper says, "I promise no one else will ever see this, you have a good night, I have some other business to take care of."

As he ends their conversation at 6:04 p.m. Mrs. Niko doesn't realize that her husband has just come in through the front door until she hears, "Honey, you home?"

She's scrambling to make sure all of the messages are deleted, none of her or Cooper's videos mistakenly got saved to her camera roll, "Yea babe, in the bathroom just finishing up, be out in a second." She has made sure there's nothing to trace her and Cooper's conversation back to each other than steps out of the bathroom.

As Brandi is walking down the hallway of her house to go greet her husband, she still has a worry in the back of her mind that Cooper may be using the videos and pictures for blackmail of some sorts. As she approaches her husband, she gives him a hug and kiss on the cheek. Acting as if what just happened in that bathroom didn't just happen, she says, "Dean, sweetheart, you hungry?"

He says, "No darling, I had a big lunch at work today. Thanks for asking, though."

She then tells her husband, "I've got a bit of a migraine, and I think I'm going to lie down for a while, but if you're hungry, I don't care one bit to fix you something real quick." Knowing in the back of her mind she was thinking she could care less if he ate or not, she just wanted to act normal for a while, especially concerned about what was going to become of this Cooper situation.

Meanwhile, back at Cooper's house, he had just laid back on his bed and can't help but to keep thinking of the Brandi Niko videos he had received moments ago. So, instead of just thinking about those videos, he decides to fantasize about them. He reaches down to his waist and pulls his shorts down to his knees, then goes into his and Mrs. Niko's messages. He pulls up Mrs. Niko's masturbation video one more time and ejaculates like it's going to be the last time he ever gets to.

Saturday, October 9th, 2021

Saturday, October 9th, 2021, it's 10:30 a.m., and Cooper Clarke has just woke up and is just sitting on the edge of his bed thinking of what he's going to do today when his phone goes off, he reaches over to his nightstand, grabs it, and it's a Facebook message from Mrs. Niko that says "Hey! Good morning, was just messaging to remind you that you needed to delete the messages, picture, and videos from yesterday. You don't want those on your phone anyway, you being my student and all. That would be taking a huge risk of getting us both in trouble."

Cooper kind of giggles at the message, then he messages her back, saying, "You're worried over nothing :) I have a spy app on my phone that I will keep that all in, and nobody will ever see it, so no worries, Mrs. Niko!"

Back at Brandi Niko's house, she is sitting at the kitchen table drinking a cup of coffee alone, still waiting on her husband to wake up when her phone goes off. "Messenger:

Cooper Clarke- You're worried over nothing :) I have a spy app on my phone that I will keep that all in, and nobody will ever see it, so no worries, Mrs. Niko!"

She reads in her mind then starts typing a message back "Worried over nothing?! I am married and I'm your college librarian, I'm pretty sure that's something to be worried about!" Brandi sends back and then sits back to wait on his reply.

Back at Cooper's house, he's up and at it getting some ball shorts, tank top, and his high tops on, about to go to the local to play some pickup basketball with a few friends and teammates.

He sees that he has a new Facebook message from his librarian, he reads it and laughs. "I promise you with everything in me, nobody on earth other than me will see these messages. Besides, I'm getting all the use I can out of these, I've already jacked off twice this morning to you, now I'm going to be busy for the next little bit, may not reply, ttyl! ;)" Cooper sends back to Brandi right before getting on the basketball court to play some pickup games.

"Ttyl? Talk to you later? Who does this kid think he is?" Brandi says to herself under her breath. So, instead of taking care of the situation they were dealing with, Cooper tells Mrs. Niko that he will talk to her later and goes on about his day. So Brandi just forgets about it and finishes her cup of coffee as she waits for her husband to get up. She drinks her last drink of coffee, puts the cup in the sink, and then goes over to sit on the couch to watch the morning news.

She's watching the news and sees details of a robbery that happened the next town over last night. "What in the world is wrong with people these days?" She mumbled to herself, not even realizing she was a pot calling the kettle black, being she was entangled in a debauchery with one of her very own college students. But I guess that just slipped her mind, or she didn't think anything at all was wrong with it.

As she continued watching the news, seeing everything going on around her, she couldn't help but to think to herself, 'what I would give to just get away from this God-forsaken garbage dumpster of a town.' She decided to just turn the television off because she was getting so frustrated over nonsense. She heard her husband coming down the hall, and she rolled her eyes at the mere thought of having to deal with him any at all today.

"Good morning, sweetheart" he said as he walked up and sat down on the couch next to her.

"Not a good morning at all, I'm going to take a shower" Brandi said back to her husband as she was walking down the hall to the master bedroom. Dean absolutely floored at her reaction to him this morning thought to himself, 'Oh boy, here we go with that childish attitude again.' So he just decided to ignore her and not even engage in her ridiculous attitude all day.

Meanwhile, back in the bedroom Brandi was still thinking of all of the messages Cooper had yet to delete from his phone, not to mention he was out with friends, probably showing them all. 'I'm just going to have to try and be crazy enough to make him delete all of those messages once and for all,' Brandi thought to herself as she sat on the edge of her bed.

She started thinking about what all had happened in just the span of less than 24 hours and thought she should actually be trying to work things out with her husband since they have such a history together. At the same exact time, she also kept her mind on a big change in her life, as in get away from her husband and skip town, possibly with Cooper Clarke. But then she would come back to reality and realize how much of a long shot that could be to happen and work out.

She finally got agitated enough and tired of sitting in the bedroom, getting depressed that she just wanted to do something. She got up off the bed, made it, took the dirty laundry basket into the utility room, threw them in the washer, and started it up. She then opened the hallway closet, took out the vacuum, and started vacuuming the whole house. She had made it to the living room, where her husband was still just sitting on the couch. 'Of course, still not doing a thing as always,' she thought to herself as she said in an agitated tone, "Move your feet so I can vacuum under them. I'm trying to get this house clean if you don't mind."

"Oh, I'm sorry, you need any help, sweetheart?" Asked Dean. "No, I don't need any help, and don't call me sweetheart"

Brandi said back to him, "You just sit there and watch your TV all day."

Dean, sitting on the couch looking at her with a confused facial expression, said, "You don't have to be a smart aleck, I was just asking if you needed any help."

"Well, I don't, so just leave me alone," Brandi said, still aggravated over the fact that her student Cooper Clarke, who put the fear of them getting caught in her, was ignoring her. So she finished her vacuuming up and threw the vacuum back into the closet with force, then went back in the bedroom and lay down scrolling through Facebook. Dean still sat in the living room, still confused as to what in the world the problem was, picked up a newspaper off the end table, and started working a crossword puzzle.

Brandi had messaged Cooper again, "Just message me when you get done, we really need to talk!" Then she deleted the messages, hid her phone under the pillow so her husband wouldn't be snooping through it, and ended up dozing off.

Hours after the vacuum incident, working a crossword puzzle, being a bit puzzled himself. Dean had looked at his phone to see how fast time was flying by. It was already 2:15 p.m. he decided that he was going to take a short drive down the road to the bookstore to see if they had any books of interest to him. He got in his truck and left.

Brandi had woken up from the sound of him shutting the front door and came into the living room to peep out the window to see what he was doing. He was backing out of the driveway leaving, "Thank God!" she yelled out to herself, pleased to see he was gone and she had the house to herself.

She used the free time she had alone to go into the bedroom, strip all of her clothes off, and masturbate to Cooper Clarke's Facebook pictures until she got off. She got done, cleaned herself up, lay back down on the bed, and turned on Wheel of Fortune.

She was watching her TV show when she got a hankering for a snack, she headed to the kitchen and fixed herself a bowl of frosted flakes, headed back into her room with her cereal, and continued watching her show.

Meanwhile, a few miles across town, at the "Stook Bore" bookstore (Yes, that's what it was called), Dean was looking through the fantasy section, trying to find something of interest, not yet realizing for certain that his wife was living a fantasy of her own. He was skimming through the titles for 30 minutes or longer until he found the brand new novel "A Spindle Splintered" By Alix E. Harrow that was just been released 4 days prior. He was a sucker for a great, weird fantasy read, and that's exactly what it was. He bought the book and left the store, heading home excited to start reading it. Before he went home, he made a pit stop at the local liquor store and picked up a bottle of red wine, he didn't drink a lot, but on some occasions, he would. He figured a glass of wine while reading his new book would help keep his mind off of what he and his wife were going through at the time. He made it back home to find his wife still in the bedroom watching TV, he didn't even waste his time trying to speak to her. He poured him a glass of wine, put the bottle in a cabinet, and sat down in his chair to start reading his book.

Back in the master bedroom, Brandi Niko was scrolling through people's Facebook once again (Forgetting that's what got this whole debacle between her and her husband started), but that aside, she was only scrolling to pass time. She came across a trailer for a movie that had been released a few months ago, and it made her want to watch it. "The River Runner"

"In this documentary, a kayaker sets out to become the first man to paddle the four great rivers that flow from Tibet's sacred Mount Kailash." She read aloud from the bio, "This seems really interesting," so she found the movie on Netflix and started watching it.

Around 4:30 p.m., her movie had ended, and she was sneaking through the house to see if her husband was home or. As she came around the corner, she saw him passed out on the recliner with an empty bottle of wine and wine glass sitting on the end table.

'Wow, had you an early night cap, didn't you' she thought to herself as she headed into the kitchen to find her a good cold Pepsi, and she maybe grabbed her a honey bun on her way back to her bedroom.

She ended up going back into her bedroom and turning on one of her favorite comedy series on Netflix "The Office," she always thought Steve Carell was a comedic genius in the show. She started the show and was already speaking with them word for word (She had only watched it from beginning to end about 6 times before). "Oh, this show never gets old," she said to herself. Hours wasting away, and by the time she thought about it, she looked in the corner of the TV, and she was just about to start season 2, episode 6! "Oh my goodness," she said to herself.

She looked at her phone, and it was already 8:15 p.m. She started rubbing her eyes and stretching her legs, getting ready to call it a night. She turned the TV off, then checked her Facebook messenger one last time to see if Cooper had ever messaged her back like he said he would, nope, nothing. She lay her phone down on her nightstand, leaned over to turn her fan on, rolled over to turn her night lamp off, lay back, and fell into a deep sleep.

Sunday, October 10th, 2021

Sunday, October 10th, 2021, it's 9:15 a.m., and Cooper Clarke has just woke up to get his day started. Of course, like any guy in the mornings, the first thing he does when his feet hits the floor is head for the bathroom. As he's standing in front of his toilet peeing, he hears it, "Ding," he just got a Facebook message. "Wonder who that could be?" he says to himself sarcastically with a chuckle and slight grin. He then shakes his penis off, making sure it's clear off all unwanted urine, then proceeds over to the sink.

He then stands in front of the sink, looking into the mirror with a cocky little grin, and says to himself, "Man, what a weekend already." He then reaches down and grabs the bar of soap, turns the hot water on, runs his hands through the water, gets his hands all lathered up, and proceeds to wash them. Then he rinses his hands off, dries them, and then grabs his toothbrush.

"Ding," another Facebook messenger notification. He chuckles again, then picks up his Crest Cinnamon toothpaste, squirts a layer across the bristles of his toothbrush, and starts brushing his teeth. "Ding," yet another Facebook message has been sent to his phone, he spits the toothpaste residue in the sink, fills his rinse cup up with water, gargles what's left in his mouth around, spits it out then cleans the sink up.

Cooper finally gets intrigued by who all of those messages are from, as if he doesn't already know, but still, he walks over to his nightstand where his phone is on charge, disconnects the chord, and opens up Facebook messenger. Wondering what all she has sent. He clicks on her name, "The one and only Brandi Niko," he says to himself. 3 unread messages from her already, and it's only 9:22 in the morning, "Ah, this is going to be a long day," he mutters to himself. He finally decides to open up the messages to see what could be so important or urgent that she has sent 3 messages back to back to back.

The first message, 9:17 a.m., "Hey, sorry to message you so early, I'm just having really bad anxiety about all of our messages from Friday evening. You never messaged me back yesterday like you said you would, about the messages though, was just wondering if you had given any thought about deleting them? The last message I got from you yesterday made it seem as if you were holding onto them. Just please tell me you've deleted them, Thanks!"

He chuckles to himself thinking of how worried she is over their little exchange of messages. On to the second message, coming in at 9:19, which reads, "So, you usually message me back fairly quickly, like as in 1 second after I send one, and it's already been 2 minutes, but yet you still haven't messaged me back. I'm starting to get frustrated, what we done was by no means 'illegal,' but I am your teacher on a college campus, and I could lose my job! Not to mention, they will make an example out of me for this. Also, which you should already know, I am MARRIED!! I will lose my husband, my home, and any friend I've ever had over this! You BETTER DELETE those messages, ALL OF THEM! And forget this EVER happened."

By this time, Cooper was not laughing anymore, he was furious over the threats he was getting from the teacher who came on to him first. Now, 9:21, the last message she has sent in the past minute or two, Cooper starts reading it to himself.

"This is the last message that I'm going to send you, begging you to delete those messages, I'm sorry that I kind of lost my temper in the last message, I'm just really worried that this isn't going to end well for either of us, I don't really have the time to explain in a message at the moment because my husband should be getting up any minute now and I don't want to get us caught. I'm begging you to meet me at school Monday morning at 5 a.m., which will give us around 3 hours Before school starts to come to an agreement about our problems, but you had better be prepared for surprises, never know about people showing up to work earlier than normal, so just be sure to have an excuse as to why we're the only 2 in there that early, please think about it."

After reading the message, Cooper goes back into the bathroom, lays his phone down on the sink, then starts a hot shower, gets in, and just stands as the lava-like water ran down his head, neck, and back. He stood in the shower for about 30 minutes, really giving some thought to everything his teacher Brandi had said in her messages. He had finally came to a decision, he stepped out of the shower, grabbed a towel, dried off, and then put his clothes on.

Afterward, he ran downstairs real quick to make him an egg sandwich with some of his favorite Louisiana Hot Sauce and a glass of 2% white milk. He ate his breakfast in a quick manner, then ran back up stairs and grabbed his phone off of the sink.

"It's already 10:08" he thought to himself as he was looking at how time was already flying by this morning. But even so, he knew it was finally time that he responded to Mrs. Niko. "Okay, I've given this some thought and have decided that I will meet you at 5 Monday morning to get this straightened out for the sake of your career, marriage, and reputation in the community."

Back at Mrs. Niko's house, her husband had just woken up, and again, she was disgusted at the sight of him, but she had to go on acting as if life was all normal to make everything seem picture-perfect to him. "Good morning darling, I was just about to fix me some cinnamon-sprinkled French toast and a couple fried eggs, would you like some as well?"

She asked, hoping he would say yes so she could tell him to go sit in the living room, and she would bring it to him.

"Uh, sure, I believe I would like to have some sweetheart." She grinned at him, gave him a kiss on the cheek, and said, "Go have a seat in the living room, you can watch the morning news or something, and I'll cater it to you! I love you!" Her husband replied, "Sounds like a plan, I love you too!"

"Finally!" she thought in her head as she headed to the back of the kitchen to check her phone. She opens Facebook messenger and to her surprise, Cooper has agreed to meet her Monday morning but wanted to be one hundred percent certain nobody else would be there. She blew with a sigh of relief, "Thank God," she mumbled to herself as she began typing one last message to send back.

As she started typing, "Okay, great, we will meet in the library, I have a key" Her husband had walked up behind her, "Need any help?" she heard as she was typing the message, "Oh my God" she yelled out as she dropped her phone in the floor landing face up! Her husband started looking down toward the phone, but she reached down, grabbed it up quickly, and stuck it in her pocket. Her husband said, "I'm sorry, babe," with a slight laugh. "Was you talking to somebody?"

"No, babe, I was just looking at this recipe, did you need something?"

"I was just going to tell you to slice up some bananas on my French toast," her husband said kind of confused. "Okay darling, I'll get it done, just go back and sit down, and ill surprise you with it."

So her husband went back into the living room and sat down, as he was sitting in his chair, he thought to himself something was odd about the way she was acting. Back in the kitchen, Brandi was trying to finish sending her message quickly to Cooper, "Now where was I?" She asked herself. 'Oh yeah,' she thought while starting to read and type. 'Okay, we will meet in the library, I have a key,' she read in her mind, then started back typing, "So we don't have to worry about it being locked since it's going to be so much earlier before school." She sent it back to Cooper as she headed back into the living room with breakfast for her husband.

"What are we going to do today, babe?" she asked her husband as she sat down next to him while he started wolfing down his breakfast,

"Ugh, I don't know, I was kind of wanting to go watch that new Michael Myers movie, Halloween Kills, I mean, it is October, but honestly, I don't even really care," he said, kind of irritated while shrugging his shoulders.

His wife, with a strange look on her face, wondering what his problem was, replied back, "Well, we don't have to go if you don't want to." Brandi said back to her husband, who she felt was a bit irritated for some reason.

"No, that's fine," Dean said, "Look up the show times, and if you want to go, we will go."

Brandi googled the showings up on her phone and replied back to her husband, "So it's 10:40 now, and the next showing is at 12:15, you think that's enough time for both of us to get ready?"

"Oh, most definitely," Dean Niko said as he shoved his last bite of French toast and eggs into his mouth.

"Awesome, I'm going to go ahead and take a shower real quick, and then you can get in after me" Brandi said as she was walking down the hallway to the master bedroom. "Give me about 30 minutes and head on back, I should be done by then," she yelled back to her husband.

"Okay, I'll give you enough time, then head on in to take mine." Dean yelled back to his wife. So he gave her about 25 minutes to shower, then headed into the bedroom to take his.

About the time he stepped into the master bathroom, he heard her phone go off, so he just leaned over and glanced at it. "Messenger: Cooper Clarke-What are we..." was what Dean saw on her phone when she suddenly slid the shower curtain open.

"Oh my God, honey, you're going to have to quit sneaking up on me like that!" Brandi said while grabbing her phone off the sink in a quick manner.

"Sorry babe, didn't mean to scare you, but who is Cooper Clarke?" Brandi, with her heart racing as she was stepping out of the shower, thought quickly,

"That's one of my students asking what assignment they're supposed to do this weekend."

Dean thought to himself, 'Assignments? You're a librarian', but he didn't say anything, just shrugged it off and said, "Well let me get in there real quick."

As soon as he pulled the curtain back over him, his wife stood there typing a message back, Dean kind of peaked through the shower curtain, looking at her face and noticing a huge grin on her face as she was typing, thinking to himself, 'Something is going on, I can feel it' but just went on with his shower. Meanwhile, outside of the shower, she read the message, "What are we going to do when we meet?"

Brandi was typing a message back to Cooper, "Listen, Monday morning, when we meet, we will go from there, and we really need to quit with the messages, my husband is very suspicious."

"Okay, I'm so sorry, I won't message anymore and will see you Monday." Cooper sent back. Brandi deleted the messages, walked out of the bathroom, threw her phone down on the bed, and went in the closet to look for some clothes.

By this time, Dean had finished his shower, then got out, went ahead, brushed his teeth and hair, then headed into the bedroom to put on some clothes.

As he walked into the bedroom, he noticed his wife's phone laying on the bed, normally, he wouldn't peep inside it, but he just felt something wasn't right. He stepped over, peaked in the closet, Brandi was in there singing, still digging through hundreds of outfits, so he stepped back, grabbed the phone real quick, and unlocked it. He went straight to the Facebook messages but didn't see one message from anyone by the name of Cooper Clarke. He thought to himself, 'Is my wife deleting messages that are supposedly only questions about an assignment between her and a student? Or is their conversation something entirely different?' But he shelved these thoughts in the library of his mind and saved them for another time.

Brandi finally stepped out of the closet looking as beautiful as she ever had in a pink leather mini skirt, a lime green button-up shirt with 3 or 4 buttons unbuttoned at the top like always, with her blonde hair curled, and some lime green high heels to top the outfit off.

"How do I look, babe?" She asked her husband, who still couldn't get the message out of his mind but pushed through for now.

"Stunning, you're a doll," he said with a slight grin and wink as he walked into the closet to throw some clothes on.

"Try and find something to kind of match me," his wife said from the bedroom. He did just that but still different, he came back out with a pink Ralph Lauren polo on, the logo being lime green in color on the pocket placed on the left-hand side, and a pair of lime green dress pants. "This look alright?"

He said to his wife, "Looks awesome, babe," she said back to him as she was putting a pair of hoop earrings in her ears. He then put his deodorant, Ralph Lauren cologne, tan dress socks, brown dress shoes, and his diamond-plated watch on. "I'm ready!"

He looked down at his watch, "11:30! We better get this show on the road!" Exclaimed Dean, so he and Brandi ran out of the house, jumped in the truck, and was on their way to the theater.

They made it there around 12:08, with very few minutes to spare before the show time. Dean dropped his wife off at the door being a gentleman even though that Facebook message was still clinging on to his mind. 'Am I thinking too much into it' he thought to himself as he parked the truck and headed in himself. She was waiting on him by the ticket booth, he stopped, bought their tickets, then told her to go on in, and he'd be in right behind her after a pit stop. He stopped at the snack bar on his way through, "1 Pepsi, a Mountain Dew, box of Gobstoppers, and a large bag of popcorn," he told the employee, knowing that both he and his wife would be wanting a snack later on into the movie. He paid the cashier, grabbed their snacks, and headed into screen 2, where Halloween Kills had begun showing.

As he started down the aisle, trying to see where his wife had taken a seat, he finally saw her blonde hair lit up in the dark from her phone light. 'Of course, she's on her phone,' he thought to himself as he got closer behind her. As he got behind her, he saw that she had Facebook messenger pulled up, he started trying to look at her phone, but she must have heard him behind her because she locked her phone real quick and reach out to grab her pop.

"Sorry honey, I was checking my work email to make sure they hadn't sent out anything about the new books I had placed an order for." He kind of just sat there with a blank stare on his face as he thought to himself, 'Why all the lies, I know for a fact you just lied,' but instead of causing another argument, he just said, "Oh yea, they sent anything about them yet?"

"Nope, still waiting" she said with a grin. For the remainder of the night, Dean sat there trying to enjoy the new movie but could not because all he could think about was his wife deliberately lying straight to his face. About 20 minutes into the movie, Brandi turns to her husband.

"Oh was you wanting to know about what happened before you made it in here? It wasn't much, really." Dean, with that annoyed look on his face once again, "Oh no, I probably seen it in the trailer honestly, I don't care that I missed it."

Brandi rolling her eyes as she turned away from him, knowing in her mind that something else had caused a sour attitude this afternoon. So, instead of trying to engage in any conversation at all with her husband, she just sat there silently enjoying the movie, letting out a shriek from being scared here and there. As so the other women and young children who sat in the audience.

About 30 more minutes went by of the movie, and Dean noticed his wife lit her phone up, looked at the time, sighed, and flipped her phone back face down as if she was irritated. "Are you not enjoying the movie or something? I mean, we didn't have to come tonight if you really didn't want to." Dean said to his wife in an aggravated manner.

"Dean, just because I check the time on my phone doesn't mean that I didn't want to come to watch the movie, quit being so pettish over every little thing."

Dean, with a confused but angry look on his face, said, "I was being pettish. I was just making sure this is what you"

"Just shut up, I have to go to the bathroom, or am I allowed?" Brandi said to Dean, cutting him off from finishing what he was saying.

"No, be my guest, go to the bathroom, I'll be waiting." Dean said back to his wife furiously under his breath as she got up and stormed out of the screening room.

Just as soon as she made it in the bathroom, Facebook messenger got pulled up, and she clicked on Cooper Clarke's name, she couldn't resist. "Hey, I'm at the movies with my husband, and just being around him infuriates me anymore, I just want to be away from him, but I don't know what to do."

Back at Cooper's house, he had just fixed him a sandwich and headed back into his bedroom to find that he had a new Facebook message, he picked his phone up and saw the message, "Mrs. Niko?!" he said to himself, very surprised.

He read the message aloud to himself and started replying back, "Listen, we will just stick to the initial plan of meeting at the school tomorrow morning, I really feel as if everything will go alright, nobody will be there. But I have got to go, my husband is calling me."

As she starts to walk out of the bathroom, she answers her husband's phone call, "Hello, I'm walking back out of the bathroom right now, my stomach is killing me." Knowing she's lying right through her teeth.

"Oh honey, I'm sorry, you wanting to leave or finish the movie?" ask her husband over the phone.

"I'm alright to finish, just may make another trip here, I'm walking back in now, bye." She hangs the call up with her husband and makes her way back down to her seat beside him.

"You sure you're alright, sweetie?" Dean ask Brandi as she sits down next to him.

"My stomach is rumbling a little, but I'll be alright to finish the movie." So Mr. and Mrs. Niko finished the movie and ended up getting back to their truck out of the crowded theater about 10 minutes after 2.

Brandi was sitting there, just silent, when her husband asked, "Do you want to stop and get some actual food from a restaurant before we go home?"

Brandi blew and said, "Honestly, Dean, I just want to go home, I don't feel like doing anything else but going home and laying down, can we please just go?"

Dean, not really infatuated by his wife's response, said, "You know what, that's a great idea because honestly, I'm so sick and tired of dealing with your bull crap that it's ridiculous, I don't know what's been going on with you but it needs to change, and it needs to change quick!"

Brandi just ignored her husband's response as he burnt rubber from his tires and sped off to their house. They made it home, got out of the truck, went into the house, and Brandi went to the master bedroom and slammed the door shut behind her.

Dean went over to the recliner, flopped down on it, turned the television on, and just lay back. Meanwhile, back in the bedroom, Brandi was on her phone surfing through Facebook, looking at everybody's posts, liking the ones she wanted, and so on. She then clicked on her messenger app, and what do you know, Cooper Clarke was active. Before she decided to message him, she crept into the living room to see if her husband was asleep. She peaked toward the recliner, saw him lying back, not moving, and figured he was out for the night.

She made her way back into the bedroom, picked her phone up, and sent Cooper a message. "So we are still on for Monday morning, am I right?"

Back at Cooper's house, he was in his bed asleep with a movie still playing on Netflix. He had been watching movies all night and could not stay up any longer.

So Mrs. Niko was sitting on her bed awaiting a response from Cooper when she started getting a little hungry, she snuck into the kitchen, trying her best not to wake her husband to find her a bite to eat. By this time, the hours had flown by so fast since they had been home she couldn't believe her eyes when she looked at the stove clock, and it was already 7:45 pm. She made her a tuna salad sandwich with a hand full of Doritos on the side, then headed back into her bedroom. She turned the TV on the cooking channel where the chef was teaching how to make a dish of "The Best Homemade Tacos Outside Of Mexico," so she figured she would just leave the TV on that channel. She finally remembered that Cooper had sent her a message as she reached over on her nightstand and grabbed her phone.

She read the message and then responded, "Yes, I will see you in the library at 5 a.m." then Brandi just flopped her phone down beside her as she continued watching TV. About

25 minutes later, Mr. Niko had woke back up about to use the bathroom all over himself, he jumped up off the recliner and sprinted toward the bathroom and made it just in time.

As he came out of the bathroom, he noticed his wife had fell asleep with a paper plate under her right arm and a few Doritos in the bed with her. He kind of chuckled, then started to turn and walk back into the living room, but he noticed her phone light up, and it caught his attention. 'Am I really going to be nosey?' he thought to himself, really wanting to check her phone. He didn't waste much time making his mind up that he was going to take a peek at her phone. He crept over beside the bed and picked the phone up as he thought to himself, 'She has been acting very strange and secretive here lately.' As soon as he picked the phone up, the screen lit up, and he saw it, the reason he felt like 'Something just wasn't right.'

A message came across her screen from the name he had seen on it before, "Messenger-Cooper Clarke: I can't wait to see you Monday morning before everyone gets there :)" Dean's heart absolutely shattered into a million pieces right then and there as he stood beside his wife as she was sleeping with her phone in his hand and a message from her student excited about meeting her at 5 a.m. Monday morning, hours before school even starts. He was heartbroken, he felt so alone, betrayed, like his whole life had just been ripped out from under him, but at the same time, he was angry, he was very angry! He marked the Facebook message as unread so his wife would never know he saw it, locked her phone, and lay it back down on the bed beside her.

As Dean walked out of the room, he turned back and looked at his wife one last time in disgust as she lay silently sleeping. Dean went back to sitting in his recliner, so mad he could have put water in his mouth and boiled it. For hours and hours, he just sat silently in his recliner, at some points sobbing with tears rolling down his cheeks. Not only crying from pain but crying in anger, thinking, 'How could my wife do this to me?' 'Not just with another man, but with her student!' He just kept thinking about it, to the point to where he had hatched a plan.

He got ready for work like he normally did, shower, teeth, cologne work clothes, and grabbed his diamond-plated watch he always wore. He had left a note on the refrigerator saying that his boss needed him to come into work earlier for inventory, said his boss told him to be there at 4 this morning and that he would see her this evening. But in reality, Dean Niko was sitting in his truck behind 2 other trucks on Sutter St., 3 streets down from his house, where he knew his wife would be passing by.

Monday, October 11ᵗʰ, 2021

Monday, October 11th, 2021, 5 a.m. rolls around, and Brandi's alarm clock has just went off. She crawls out of bed jumps in the shower to get ready for a day she anticipates more than normal. She's got her hair and make-up all done has her short skirts button-up shirt on with an even extra button unbuttoned today on.

She finally finishes in the bathroom and comes creeping down the hallway to the living room, where, to her surprise, her husband is already gone. She stands there for a second and thinks to herself 'Where would he be gone to so early, he doesn't have to be at work until 7, hmm' then she makes her way into the kitchen where she finds his note "Sorry darling, had to be at work at 4 this morning for inventory, see you this evening, love you" he had to make it believable as if nothing at all was wrong.

She looks at the clock, and it's already 4:30 in the morning, "Oh, I better get to get to going, I definitely don't want to be late meeting Cooper," she said to herself with a smile that almost touched each ear. So she grabs her purse, her curriculum she was supposed to be working all weekend (but couldn't because of trying to keep up with all of the lies going on in her life), and headed out the door on her way to the college.

Back on Sutter St., where Dean Niko is sitting in his truck, he sees his wife's car go by, so he waits a few seconds and then pulls out to follow her. He knows exactly where she's going, so he can stay behind as far as he needs. Up ahead is Brandi Niko in her brand new 2021 blacked-out Toyota Camry, looking in her rearview mirror, making sure her hair is still fixed and make-up is on point. She's about 10 minutes from the college, and it's already 4:40 a.m. 'I can't wait to see Cooper's reaction to me,' she thinks to herself as she takes the left turn onto Highway 99, that puts her on a straight shot going by the college. Her husband, about three-tenths of a mile behind her gritting his teeth and gripping the steering wheel so hard he feels as if he could fold it in half while he's driving.

About a half mile away from the college entrance, Brandi reaches over in her purse, gets her favorite bottle of perfume out, sprays a little on each wrist to rub together, then spread on her neck.

About 3 minutes later, she pulls into the school parking lot. As she is looking for a parking spot, she sees Cooper's red Ford truck already parked, she parks and, gets out of her vehicle, and starts walking in, she looks at the time on her phone, "It's 4:58, I sure hope he's here."

As she makes it to the side entrance door of the library, there he was, sitting on the bench waiting, Cooper Clarke. "Well, good morning, good looking," he says to Mrs. Niko as she sticks her key in the door.

"Good morning, Cooper, now get in here before anybody sees us."

By this time, Dean had just pulled into the school parking lot as well, he parks his truck about 3 spots down from his wife's car and got out. "Please, God, just let this be some type of misunderstanding of mine" he says to himself as he's walking toward the library.

As he's walking by the library windows, he looks in and sees his wife's student, Cooper Clarke, wrap his arms around her waist and start making out with her. The worst part of all, she isn't rejecting any at all. They were in between 2 book shelves hid from eyes inside the library, but from where Dean Niko was standing, he could see it all.

Mr. Niko drops to his knees outside the window and begins puking his guts up in absolute disgust at what he has just witnessed his wife take part in. He had found, seen, and dealt with enough this past weekend, he was done dealing with it. He stood up off the ground, wiped his mouth off, and busted through the same side door they had come through and yelled out, "Are you kidding me, Brandi! Really?! Your student!"

Brandi now standing there with no top or bra on, with her breast in being kissed on by Cooper, and not to mention their bottoms, with both her panties and his underwear already down to their knees. They both jumped back pulled their bottoms back up around their waist, Cooper, of course, with no shirt on.

"I can explain Dean. It's not what it looks like." Dean laughed, "Not what it looks like. Both of you were kissing, and you all close to being naked! How is it not what it looks like? I'm going to ki…"

He couldn't even finish his sentence when Cooper came at him full force with a knife and stabbed him in the rib cage.

"Oh my God, Cooper, no!" Brandi yelled out, but it was already too late, he had already brought the knife from the rib cage up to the throat and slit Dean Nikos throat wide open.

"What have you done, Cooper? What have you done?" Brandi Niko screamed with a screech that would raise the dead.

"What do you mean what have I done? I was protecting us! When we talked Saturday, you told me I had better be prepared for surprises. Well, that was me being prepared."

"Yeah, I meant a story to back up what we were both doing here if we heard somebody coming in, not you murdering my husband!" Brandi shouted out to Cooper.

"Well, the damage is done now, Mrs. Niko, we have to do something with him, or we will be spending our life together for sure, in prison!" Cooper yelled toward Brandi Niko, who was standing there processing what had just happened.

"Okay, let me think, uh, uh, go to the janitor's closet and grab a jug of Clorox, vomit powder, some towels, and the vacuum, and you better run. We don't have much time at all. It's already 6:00, we have to move quickly!"

As Cooper left for the supplies, Brandi gave it everything she had to put her husband in an office chair and wheel him across the library into her office behind the desk. She ran back out of the office to her desk, opening and closing drawers in a rush, "Tape, Where's tape, I need tape!" she was shouting out as she was digging through her bottom drawer. She finally found a roll of tape about the time Cooper walked back through the door.

"What do I need to do?!" He shouted to his now partner in crime/librarian Mrs. Brandi Niko.

"Spread the vomit powder all over the blood first, let it soak for a few, very few seconds, then take the vacuum and go over it. Holler when you finish that," Mrs. Niko instructed Cooper. So she ran in her back office and started wrapping tape around her dead husband to be sure he didn't fall out of the chair. She heard the vacuum start and run for a few minutes, then shut off.

"Mrs. Niko, what now?" Cooper shouted.

Brandi came running out of her office, "Okay, you just go in my office there, finish putting the tape around him, be quiet, and shut the door, do not come out whatsoever until I come get you."

"Okay, got it" Cooper responded back to her as he was shutting the door behind him. Mrs. Niko grabbed the jug of Clorox and started pouring it all over the floor where the blood was. She grabbed the towel and started scrubbing the floor with everything in her might. She scrubbed and scrubbed down on her hands and knees behind the bookshelf where the killing had happened until she no longer saw blood. She then jumped up, threw all of the towels she had used into the garbage, and ran the supplies they had borrowed back down to the janitors closet.

When she got back, she went back over to where she had been cleaning up blood and started running her hands across it again to make sure she had it all cleaned up. Mrs. Niko was still in the floor trying to inspect when she looked at her phone, and it was already 6:33 a.m. and, not to mention she just realized it was Monday morning!

'Oh my God!' she thought to herself as she was still in the floor, 'there will be students coming in about 20 minutes, what are we going to do?!' she started panicking and crying as she continued scrubbing for the next couple of minutes. She heard the library door open, 'Oh my goodness,' she thought, the janitor must have opened the door for a student, she shoved all the rags she was using under the bookshelf.

6:37 a.m., Michael Michaelson had just walked into the Wheel Herd Community College library extremely earlier than usual when he noticed Mrs. Niko's feet and ankles sticking out from behind a bookshelf. He immediately ran down the aisle hastily, hoping he wasn't about to run up on his favorite librarian harmed in any manner.

Michael reached the aisle Mrs. Niko was in and found her fine and dandy, just searching for something in the floor.

"Thank God" he said to himself as he was trying to catch his breath from the start of a panic attack that was about to come on.

"Are you okay, Michael?" Mrs. Niko asked as she turned and saw him ghost faced and in a clammy manner.

"Yes" he said loudly with joy. "I came in and only saw your feet sticking out behind the bookshelf, and I thought for sure I was going to walk upon a different scene."

Mrs. Niko stood up from the floor, body slightly shaking all over, clammy, and sweaty, took her left hand and gently stroked Michael's soft, pale cheeks and said, "Thank you, Michael, for actually caring enough to actually come and check on me, I am fine though, but were you needing something?" Mrs. Niko asked, kind of nervously. "I'm kind of busy at the moment getting caught up on a couple of things before school starts."

Michael said, "No, I was just returning my book."

'Why so early?' Mrs. Niko thought to herself as Michael started walking toward the slot in the desk in front of her office where you return your books. She shouted, "Michael! Just lay that over here on the table, and I'll put that up for you, it will be easier for me to just put it back on the shelf since I'm already over here." Mrs. Niko slightly giggled after explaining.

Michael said, "Okay, sounds good," as he lay the book down on the old wobbly Cherry wood library table. Michael then walked off and left the library, kind of confused, but didn't say anything else.

As soon as she heard the exit door shut, Mrs. Niko ran down the aisle towards the door and locked the deadbolt. As soon as she locked the deadbolt she then began to dart towards her office. She flung open the door and yelled at Cooper, "We have to go, we have to get out of here now! Drop everything, forget whatever you're doing, and let's go! Shut that door behind you!"

Cooper jumped up, shut the door, ran behind her, and they left out the back door they came in through just as quick as possible. "Go jerk the license plate off the back of your car and just leave it here, we can't stop anywhere at all until we are multiple towns over," Brandi told Cooper Clarke.

Cooper did what she said, took his license plate off of the back of his car, jumped in the car with her and they left before anybody even knew they were there.

"Oh my God, What did we just do?" Shouted Brandi as they sped away, about to hit the interstate to leave town. "We done what was needed to be done, now just drive until you can't drive anymore!" Cooper shouted out.

"We just killed somebody, Cooper, you don't see a problem with that?!" Brandi shouted back at Cooper.

Cooper got agitated shouted back, "Yes, I see a problem with it, but it's done, it's over with, there isn't a thing we can change now, so just keep driving, besides you're the one who knew to make sure everything was cleaned up, get my license plate off my car, so don't go saying what have we done now."

So the two of them just drove and just kept driving. Mrs. Niko looked over at Cooper at one point, and he was dead asleep. She smacked him on the shoulder, "If I can't sleep, neither can you!"

"We have to sleep, Brandi! I'll sleep while you drive, and you can sleep while I drive. It's 8 a.m. drive until you just can't drive any longer. Wake me up when you can't hold your eyes open anymore, and I'll drive."

So she did just that. She drove until she could barely hold her eyes open. 'Surely I've been driving for 12 or 13 hours,' she thought to herself. She got about to use the bathroom all over herself when she saw a sign that read "Gas Station-5 Miles." she thought to herself, 'Thank God, I can't hold it no longer, now if I could just find out where the heck I am.' She drove about 2 or 3 more miles until she saw another sign come up: "Welcome to Amarillo, Texas."

"Oh, my goodness she shouted out," waking Cooper up out of his nap. "What's going on?!" He shouted out, kind of scared. "It's already 7:45 p.m. we're already in Texas, that far away from my home already, what have we done?"

"We done what was right, hey, there's a gas station coming up ahead, pull over there so we can use the bathroom, get some food, and I'll drive awhile so you can get some sleep, that's probably what's wrong with you," Cooper said to Brandi, just trying to calm her down and get her mind off things.

So she did just that, she pulled into the gas station, they both went straight for the bathrooms, then she grabbed her a hotdog, Milky Way, and a Pepsi. Cooper went for a bag of Doritos, Mountain Dew, and a slice of gas station pizza.

They sat down in a little booth inside the gas station, ate their food, and headed back out, this time with Cooper behind the wheel.

Cooper turned the radio on at a low volume so it wouldn't wake Brandi, by this time, it was 9:00 p.m., and as soon as he turned the radio on, he heard, "In other news, a body of a middle-aged man has been found in the library of the College Of Southern Nevada, we'll have more on that at 11." His jaw almost hit the floorboard of the car. 'Oh my God, he thought to himself' as he just kept driving, praying that Brandi hadn't overheard. Considering he believed she was already having regrets of all that has happened anyway.

Cooper got to thinking about all that had went down this morning and realized that eventually, they're going to put 2 and 2 together when they, '1. Find his truck in the back parking lot, even though he took the license plate, somebody will know it's his, 2. When they realize that Mrs. Niko is not at school or home, and her husband is dead in the library of the school. Last but not least, 3. When they check the school cameras in the back parking lot and see them fleeing together.' Cooper thought and thought on everything going on for the next hour or so of driving, 'If we can make it far enough, we can just come up with new identities and start life fresh.' 'I don't think they're going to look for us forever, especially multiple states over, just need to stay calm and not worry,' he told himself.

11 p.m. rolls around, and the news broadcast comes across the radio, "Breaking News out of Southern Nevada earlier today, a body has been found in the library of the

College Of Southern Nevada. Police have evidence that the body is Dean Niko, the husband of the Southern Nevada college librarian, who is nowhere to be found at the moment, Brandi Niko. Also, police have located a red Ford truck in the back parking lot behind the library believed to be owned by star point guard, well-known honor student Cooper Clarke, which was not at school today but, even more unlike him, didn't show up to basketball practice. This belief comes from students saying they know who the car belongs to, but a missing license plate keeps us from knowing that to be one hundred percent true. It is a very great possibility that this car does, in fact, belong to Mr. Clarke because along with Mrs. Niko, he has yet to be found. We'll keep you updated as this investigation is ongoing."

So Cooper had been driving for another hour and a half when he started getting a little sleepy, hoping that Brandi would soon wake up from her nap so they could switch seats.

On the passenger side, Brandi had heard every word that came over the radio from the news broadcast that went on air at 11 p.m. She lay there and couldn't quit thinking about it. 'They know what we've done, oh my God, his car is still there, and they're going to find us.' She just lay there motionless, hoping Cooper couldn't tell that she was actually awake. "Aww," Cooper yawned as he rubbed his eyes, "So tired," he said aloud, at this time, Brandi had finally decided to wake up to let him sleep so she could do a whole lot of thinking about what has transpired over less than 24 hours.

She came to, yawning and stretching as if she was actually asleep, and said with a fake half-asleep voice, "If you're tired, I can drive for a while. I'm all rested up, I'm so sorry, I didn't even realize you had been driving as long as you have."

"Oh, Okay."

"It's going on 11:30 p.m. right now, I'll drive to the next small town I see and pull over, I say small town because I'd like to find an actual restaurant to get some good food from, gas station food is old." Cooper replied back with a slight laugh.

Brandi replied back, barely looking him in the eye due to worries, "Sounds good to me. Just wake me up if I'm asleep when we get there." She closed her eyes and lay there just thinking about what they had done, and the fact that everyone knew made it worse. Cooper drove for about another hour and a half while Brandi layover in the passenger seat and "slept."

All Brandi could think about, though, was what the news was saying, and she just knew that the next stop they made, the police were probably going to be waiting to arrest them, 'I'm sure authorities all over the country have been informed to be on the lookout.' She thought to herself as she lay there pretending to still sleep. "Wake up, sleepy head!" Cooper yelled out to Brandi, "We're in Oklahoma City, Oklahoma!"

"Oh my goodness, be quiet," Brandi said, slightly giggling but really meaning it. Brandi, wandering where they were actually going on this journey and just trying to get a conversation going with Cooper.

"Doesn't your favorite NBA basketball player play in this town?" Brandi, referring to Kevin Durant.

"No, he left for the Golden State Warriors, played with them 3 seasons, then went to the Brooklyn Nets, stayed there awhile, then headed on to the Phoenix Suns," Cooper replied back.

"Oh, I did not know that, but I knew you would for sure, you want to stop and get something to eat real quick, and maybe and maybe a change of clothes?" Brandi asked Cooper.

Cooper replied back, "Yeah, there's a Wal-Mart right up the road there, we can run in there real quick and get back out. There shouldn't be many people inside, considering it's almost midnight."

Brandi thought in the back of her head, 'Yeah, until we go inside and theirs a police officer making his rounds or something,' but she didn't say that, and instead just replied back, "Yea, but if we go in, we better make it as quick as possible, and try not to be seen by anybody."

"We will! In and out really quick," Cooper said back in an excited tone.

Tuesday, October 12th, 2021

It's now Tuesday, October 12th, 2021, and about 15 minutes later, they pulled into the Walmart parking lot that was completely empty, "An empty Walmart parking lot at any time of the day is kind of weird, right?" Cooper asked Brandi who was staring out the window of the car.

"Yeah, I guess it is."

"Surely it's not closed, is it?" Cooper asked Brandi as he was driving through the deserted Walmart parking lot. They finally make it up to the doors, and theirs a sign on the door that reads.

"Due to shortage of night shift stocker, we now close the store at 11 p.m. sorry for any inconvenience."

As they were sitting in front of the door reading the sign, they didn't realize that a police officer had pulled up behind them and was running their plates. "Yeah, dispatch, I need you run Alpha, Delta, Romeo 7 2 3"

"Yes, sir, that comes back to a Brandi Niko out of Henderson, Nevada, and sir, there is an APB out on her in that area."

"Dispatch 10-23, I'm in the Wal-Mart parking lot with this vehicle, 20 is 1801 Belle Isle Blvd, 10-12 for anything further."

"10-4 Sir." Back in the car with Brandi and Cooper, he has just looked in his drive-side mirror and noticed the cop getting out of the vehicle and walking towards the car. "Oh my God, Brandi, there's a cop walking up to my window right now, he's about 10 feet from. What should I do? Tell me now!"

But as soon as he said those last words, he couldn't wait on her response any longer, he put the car in reverse, stomped on the gas, hit the police cars front end with his rear end, immediately put it back up into drive, stepped on the gas and took off like a bad out of hades, trying to get out of that parking lot as fast as he possibly could.

Meanwhile, the officer had turned around and was running back to his vehicle to dispatch back to the station that they had run. "What are you thinking?!" Brandi screamed at Cooper, "You have just screwed us, we are destroyed now, and that cop could've been just going to ask us if we needed any help or just going to tell us that the store was closed, and when did all we would've had to say was okay, we will just come back tomorrow, but no, you had to go all psycho and hit his vehicle! You are stupid! He was just doing his job, now they are going to be looking for us! We might as well turn ourselves in at this point!"

Brandi was so furious, punching the dashboard and kicking the floorboard, all Cooper could think was how right she actually was, but there was no way he was turning himself in.

Cooper fled out of the parking lot and was on route 40 in a matter of a couple of minutes. "We're just going to do like we were initially supposed to do in the first place, just drive, drive, and drive. I told you stopping at that Wal-Mart was a horrid idea. Now look at us, trying to escape the cuffs of the law. Look what you have caused!"

Wednesday, October 13th, 2021

"Here it is 12:30 a.m., and I'm driving insane speeds just to hope we can get far enough away from this area before the police catch up." So Cooper just kept driving for about an hour or 2 until Brandi finally asked,

"Are you tired? I know you have to be, it's already 2:30 in the morning, want you find a secluded bridge, pull under it, and lets sleep and hold each other, please."

Brandi was just trying to get him to slow down because it was starting to scare her, in the back of her mind, she was regretting everything more and more every second that passed by. 'How did I even get mixed in with him? He was my student, what was I thinking? I was married to a great husband, I was just looking for reasons to get away from him because I had a young man who was giving me attention, I have absolutely destroyed my life.' All of these thoughts flooded her mind as Cooper continued driving and would not stop.

"Where are we even at?" Brandi asked Cooper as they continued driving in the pitch-black dark of the earliest hours of morning.

"Honestly, I don't even know, just lay back, be quiet, and when I come across a sign, I will let you know." Brandi rolled her eyes, sighed, and lay her seat back to try and take a nap.

About another 10 minutes went by, and Brandi had just barely started falling asleep when Cooper yelled out, "Sallisaw! Sallisaw!"

Absolutely scared the life out of Brandi, her whole body shook, she rose up out of the chair and yelled, "What are you yelling about?! You just about gave me a heart attack, are you stupid?!"

Cooper replied back, "You told me to tell you where we were when found out we are in Sallisaw, Oklahoma."

Brandi, rubbing her eyes, trying to be fully awake and get control of her breath from the near-death experience he had just gave her, said, "You mean to tell me we aren't even out of Oklahoma City yet, and you're yelling at me telling me where we are?"

'How dumb can he really be?' She thought to herself as Cooper replied back, "You told me to let you know where we are when I saw a sign, you don't have to be a smart alec and just straight butthole about me letting you know, from now on, I won't let you know a dang thing about where we are or what we're going to be doing!"

Brandi was furious, rose up even more out of her chair, pointed her finger in his face, and said, "You will tell me every little thing about this trip we're on if you so much as see a newspaper lying in a trash can that says one word even close to about why we are where we are you will tell me, do you understand me?"

Cooper just rolled his eyes at her, "Yes, I understand you, I'm just saying. There's a bridge coming up, I'm going to stop under it and take a leak real quick, I'm about to bust."

So Cooper pulled the car over and got out to relieve himself. In the car, Brandi was thinking to herself, 'This kid has to go, I can't do this anymore with him, I would rather be in my husband's position.'

Cooper came, got back in the vehicle, and said, "Alright, let's get out of here before somebody gets suspicious."

"You want me to drive for a while?" Brandi asked Cooper before they took off from under the bridge.

"Yea, go ahead, I'm going to nap a bit while you drive." So Brandi jumped over in the passenger seat and took out from under the bridge. She got back out onto the highway and began their journey of the road life once again, she got to thinking again about her husband and how what happened to him shouldn't have ever happened.

She actually got teary-eyed thinking about it and just pure out depressed. She started thinking about how, towards the end, he was trying so hard to save their marriage and how she really should have never got caught up in her lustful behavior with her college student.

She ate right into his hand, she done exactly what he wanted her to do, and what makes it worse, they didn't even get the chance to have sex, and now, even though they had been in a car for days together, they've still not had the chance.

She stopped thinking for a second and looked at the radio. It was already 4:30 a.m. 'Oh my goodness' she thought to herself, then she noticed a sign coming up, and as she got closer, the sign read "Little Rock Arkansas-25 Miles"

"Arkansas," she thought to herself 'Where has my life gone? What am I doing here? I can't do this anymore, something has to happen, and it has to happen soon.' Cooper Keeps driving along the highway as he says, "Just about to enter another state together! Little Rock, Arkansas, coming right up!" as he laughs and looks over at Brandi, who has an unpleasant look on her face.

"What's wrong, darling?" Cooper ask Brandi.

"Ahh, nothing really, I'm just really tired and would love to be able to sleep in an actual bed soon." So that gets Cooper kind of depressed that he hasn't thought about caring enough to stop and get a hotel room for them to actually get a good night's sleep.

So, after thinking about it, Cooper finally said, "Help me start looking for hotel signs, and we will get a room for the night, and since it's so early, we will be able to get it literally all day today and tonight."

Brandi gave a slight smile and said, "Okay, that sounds so awesome to me." Knowing in the back of her mind she really had other thoughts, she was basically depressed at this point in her life. She looked over at the clock on the stereo system, and it was already 5 a.m. She just blew, rolled her head back over, and closed her eyes.

About 5 minutes later, she heard, "We have now entered into Little Rock, Arkansas! So exciting!" Brandi was just completely ignoring Cooper at this point.

"I'm going try and get off of I-630 as quickly as I can, I saw signs for hotels a few miles back, so we should be in a bed soon, darling!" Brandi, with an unenthusiastic tone, replied back, "Sounds great, can't wait!"

"Or we don't have to sleep in a bed tonight, Brandi, I mean, what's your deal?"

"Cooper!" Brandi yelled back with a tone that would shake homes, "We have been in this car for 2 days now! I'm tired! I need a bath, I need a bed, find a hotel, now!"

Cooper started looking anxiously and in a hurry out of the windshield of the car, "Uh, uh, I'm looking, there, there, the, the Marriot, I can see the sign from here, I'll pull down there and get us a room real quick."

So Cooper finally pulls off the exit ramp onto S Chester St. and just starts heading toward the giant Marriot Hotel sign, they started down the street, and as the sign started getting closer, Cooper started looking for streets that lead right up to the hotel, they had drove to a W Markham St, he took a right-hand turn and finally pulled into the hotel parking lot.

Brandi told Cooper, "Just sit here in the car, I'll go get us a room. Both of us definitely don't need to be seen together, we're probably all over the news."

Cooper told her that was fine and she went on in. When she got to the desk, she told the clerk, "I need a room for 3 nights for 2 people. Also, is there a place to buy a handgun close by, I was wanting to surprise my boyfriend in the morning."

The clerk, acting a bit nervous, handed her a few papers and said, "Yes, it's unmarked on a map, but theirs one 3 blocks down the road here, but just go sit there at the desk, and you can fill those out for me, then bring them back."

Brandi said thanks and went over to the desk to fill the papers out. While Brandi was doing that, she had no clue that the clerk had recognized her from the news. Jessica, the nervous clerk, in the back office with her manager, "Michelle, I'm pretty sure that's that teacher from Nevada that's been on the run with that student for the questioning about the body of her husband that was found in that college library out in Nevada."

Michelle, the hotel manager, asked, "Jess, are you absolutely positive that's her?"

"Yes, Michelle, I know it is, step in the doorway and take a look at her, and I'll pull her picture up on the Computer."

Michelle replied back, "Okay," and stepped in the doorway to take a look at her, she got a good look at her, stepped back in the office, and took a look at the picture that Jessica had pulled up on the computer.

Michelle took one look at the picture and said, "Yes, that is certainly her, just go back out, act like everything is normal, and I'll alert the authorities after we have gave them enough time to get to their room and settled in so that they can't have a chance to run, but we have to act like everything is normal."

Jessica replied back, "Okay," so she walked back out to the desk, Brandi walked the papers back up to her and said, "There you go, all done."

Jessica told her, "Thanks, you will be in room 165, here is your keys, you guys have a great stay."

Brandi said thanks and headed back out to the car, "Okay, I got us a room, it's just right down this way, 165."

So they found their room went in to get settled in, Cooper took his shoes off and said, "I'm going to sleep, Brandi, I can't hold my eyes open any longer."

So Cooper crawled in the bed and was fast to asleep. Brandi used the bathroom real quick and quietly snuck out of the hotel room and started down the street towards the gun shop she had asked the clerk about. She had looked at a clock on a bank sign across the road, and it was 6:03 a.m.

"Time is absolutely flying by," she said to herself, "I sure hope this place is open."

So she finally made it down to the pawn shop, "Pawnshop?!" She said aloud to herself, "I was thinking she was pointing me toward an actual firearms dealer, well, I don't care. Hopefully, they have something."

So Brandi finally made it to the shop, and to her surprise, they were open, so she steps inside, and the owner says, "Good morning, my name is Tony, can I help you find something?"

She gave a slight giggle and said, "I really don't know exactly what I'm looking for, I just want to surprise my boyfriend with a pistol for his birthday, not really looking to spend a whole lot, being this will be his first gun and all." With a slight giggle and a hair twirl.

Tony gave a slight laugh and said, "I have this Hi-Point 9mm with an 8-round clip capacity and then one in the chamber I'll sale you for, oh, say, hundred fifty bucks cash."

"I'll take it!" responds Brandi quickly and excited, "Is their anyway you can throw in a clip full of bullets as well? I'm wanting to take him to a gun range later today to shoot some."

Tony smiled and said, "Sure, I'll load it up for you, by the way did you walk down here?"

Brandi replied back, "Yes, but I'm just a few blocks up the road here."

Tony kind of shook his head and said, "You're new in town here, right?"

Brandi said, "Yes, I am, why you ask?"

"Well, mam, this is kind of a dangerous neighborhood, to be quiet honest with you, but it is still early, so you will probably be just fine walking back, but just in case, come over and let me show you how to turn the safety off and be ready to fire."

So Tony showed her how to have the gun ready to fire, and before she left, she asked one more question, "So Tony, when I get it ready to fire, and then shoot, will it be ready to shoot again directly after?"

Tony replied back, "Yes, it will be, you be safe out there."

Brandi turned and walked out of the shop and headed back towards the hotel. She made it back into her and Cooper's room went in, no surprise to her, finding Cooper still asleep.

On the other hand, the clerks in the front office had called the law about 5 minutes before Brandi had left the gun shop, so more than likely, they were probably about to get a knock at the door. Brandi sat down in a chair on the far side of the room with the gun in her hand but hid under her shirt, just waiting and contemplating. 'Am I really going to do this? Is this really what needs to be done? We've both destroyed our lives anyway, so what does it really matter anymore?'

About 5 minutes into her sitting there thinking about everything, all she heard was "BOOM BOOM BOOM."

"Police, open up!" Cooper woke up out of a dead sleep! "Oh my God, they've got us Brandi. What are we going to do?!"

Brandi replied back, with tears in her eyes and a lump in her throat, "Cooper, we have had some good times, but at the same time, we have destroyed each others lives, and the bad thing is, we didn't even get to have sex because of being on the run, that was the whole point of this interaction from the get-go."

"BOOM BOOM BOOM"

"Police, we're only going to say it one more time, open up!"

Brandi continued, "This was just a fatal attraction, everything about us being attracted to each other has ended fatal," while standing up with the gun in her hand, Cooper yelled. "Brandi, what are you doing?!"

Brandi cocked the gun, aimed it at Cooper, and said, "This is the end, how poetic."

The police started kicking the door in, Brandi raised the gun up towards Cooper, aimed at his head, and pulled the trigger. "Bang" Cooper dropped to the floor as his blood flooded the hotel carpet.

Brandi then stuck the gun to her temple. The police finally busted the door open and yelled, "Put the gun down! Put the gun down now!" Brandi yelled out, "It was nothing but a fatal attraction!!" And pulled the trigger.

About the Author

Arlin Couch is a 31-year-old writer from Southeastern Kentucky, a country boy raised on a dirt road holler. His love for writing began in the sixth grade with short stories and poetry. As a teenager, he expanded into creating small books for fun and later explored songwriting, focusing on meaningful rap lyrics. Although his music career never took off, Arlin's passion for writing remained strong.

In 2023, he committed to writing his first full-length book, carving out time from his busy work schedule to bring his story to life. By 2024, he completed the manuscript and partnered with Franklin Publishers. He is now excited to introduce his debut novel, Fatal Attraction, to readers everywhere.